This book
belongs to

....

Published in 2010
by Igloo Books Ltd
Cottage Farm
Sywell
NN6 0BJ
www.igloo-books.com

C005 0210
10 9 8 7 6 5 4 3 2 1
ISBN: 978 1 84852 659 4

Project Managed by Insight Design Concepts Ltd.
Printed and manufactured in China

A Princess's Secret Wish

igloo

It was Princess Sophie's birthday and her godmother had sent her a special present.

'To Sophie,' said the label on the package.

Open this box and look inside,
there's a special locket where you can hide
secret wishes, written by you.
Then wait and they'll magically all come true.'

Princess Sophie opened the box. Inside, just as the note said, there was a beautiful, heart-shaped locket.

Wondering if the locket really could make wishes come true,
Princess Sophie found some paper and a pencil. In small, neat
letters, she wrote:
'I wish I could have cupcakes for breakfast.'
She folded her note and slipped it inside the locket. Then, she put
on the locket and, ignoring the rest of the presents piled up in her
bedroom, ran downstairs.

'Happy Birthday, Your Highness,' said the palace butler, when Sophie sat down at the breakfast table. She held her breath as he carried out the silver tray that usually held sausages or porridge. 'Raspberry cupcakes, Your Highness,' said Butler, placing the tray in front of her. 'With chocolate sprinkles.'

Princess Sophie was so surprised, she almost fell off her throne.

As soon as she had finished breakfast, Princess Sophie went back to her turret-top bedroom. She had some serious thinking to do about her next wish. Everyone in the palace was busy preparing for her birthday party and, as she heard them bustling about, it gave her an idea.

She wrote her wish on a scrap of paper, then put it inside the locket.

'I wish for fireworks at my birthday party.'

The royal birthday party was a terrific success. Princess Sophie and her friends danced and played games and drank pink lemonade. As everyone sang 'Happy Birthday', there was a sudden 'bang!' outside the palace windows. The sky was filled with fireworks, and Princess Sophie smiled. Her second wish had come true.

That night, Princess Sophie found it hard to fall asleep. She sat up in bed, staring at the magic locket on her dressing table. Could it hurt to make one more wish? She crept across the room in her bare feet. 'I wish it could be my birthday every day,' she wrote on a tiny piece of paper.

I wish it could be my birthday every day

Carefully, she slipped her wish inside the locket and climbed back into bed.

'Presents!' said Sophie, opening her eyes the next morning.

There was a huge pile of shiny, wrapped gifts at the end of her bed, just as there had been the day before.

Princess Sophie was amazed. It truly was her birthday all over again!
She ate more cupcakes, played more party games and enjoyed the
fireworks even more than she had the first time. Birthdays, she
decided as she fell asleep that night, were the best thing ever.

The following day, after she'd opened her newest pile of birthday presents, Princess Sophie went to find the King.

'May I go for a pony ride?' she asked.

'Absolutely not,' said the King. 'Your party guests will be here soon. You must be ready when they arrive.'

Princess Sophie frowned. She wanted to be outdoors with her pony, not stuck inside playing party games.

'Can I have toast this morning?' Princess Sophie asked Butler at breakfast the next morning.

'These cupcakes are a special birthday treat, Your Highness,' said Butler, putting down the silver tray.

Princess Sophie scowled. She wanted toast and marmalade, not cupcakes again.

Birthdays, Princess Sophie decided as she fell asleep that night, were fun. Playing the same games over and over again was not. Neither was eating cupcakes all the time. She was even starting to get tired of fireworks.

After a whole week of birthdays, Princess Sophie was royally miserable. With birthday celebrations every day, she couldn't ride her pony, or go to ballet lessons, or do any of the things she normally enjoyed. Her bedroom was so full of presents, there wasn't even room to play any more.

She was also worried. If every day was her birthday, did that mean all other holidays were cancelled? What about the fabulous summer ball that was held at the palace every year?

Princess Sophie felt as though she had nothing to look forward to,
except more cupcakes and party games.

'I wish everything would go back to normal,' thought Princess
Sophie. And then she remembered the locket.

She hunted through the enormous pile of presents in her bedroom
until she finally found the heart-shaped locket.

'I wish for just one birthday a year,' she wrote in her neatest, smallest handwriting.
She folded up the note and put it inside the locket. Then, she tucked the locket under her pillow and fell asleep.

I wish
for just one
birthday
a year

When she woke up the next morning, there were no new presents in her bedroom.

Princess Sophie smiled.

'Toast and marmalade, your highness,' said Butler, putting the silver tray down when she arrived at the breakfast table.

Princess Sophie smiled again.